Here You Are

"No one doubts that he exists, though you may doubt the existence of God. If you find out the truth about yourself and discover your own source, this is all that is required."

Ramana Maharshi

Text and Illustrations Copyright © 2007 by Mayke Beckmann Briggs

Summary: A small child journeys through the most fundamental truths and questions of life until realizing the ultimate truth in the end.

Printed in China

Library of Congress Control Number: 2006910917

www.BoathouseBooks.com

ISBN# 9780977646913

Here You Are

Text and Illustrations by

Mayke Beckmann Briggs

BOATHOUSE BOOKS

For You

Here you are,

standing on the ground,

under the big blue sky,

among the trees,

the flowers, and the butterflies.

Here you are,

with the clouds above you,
and the wind blowing in your hair,

with the sun
warming your face,
the air smelling sweet,

and the birds singing their songs.

Here you are,

and everything is so great, and so beautiful!

Here you are,
wondering,

"Who made everything?"

and,

"Why am I here?"

Here you are,
wondering,
about day and night,

darkness and light,

animals and trees,
friends and enemies,
about winter and summer,
sunshine and rain,

about mountains and oceans,
earthquakes and hurricanes,
loud and quiet,
bitter and sweet.

Here you are,
wondering,

about sad and happy,
weak and strong,
fearing and wishing,

and wisdom and foolishness…

Here you are,
wondering,

how everything appears out of nowhere,
like the waves rise up from the sea,

and how everything vanishes,
into nothing,

like the waves, on a calm summer's day,
into the mirror-like lake.

Here you are,
wondering,

"Who am...I?"

"Where do I come from?"
and…"Where do I go?"

Here you are…

wondering...

until suddenly,

you remember,
the forever, free and true,
the sweetest, deepest, and most quiet,
love of all,

So Big!
…in the very center of your heart,

and you smile,
and you are happy,
for…

"Here you are!"

heaven and earth ~ mystery and truth ~ desire and fear ~ beginning and end ~ darkness and light ~ good and evil ~ havi
and not having ~difficult and easy ~ high and low ~ front and back ~ bragging and humility ~ empty and full ~ weakn
and strength ~ knowledge and ignorance ~ aversion and attraction ~ dull and sharp ~ clear and fuzzy ~ coming and goin
staying and leaving ~ wisdom and foolishness ~ form and formlessness ~ giving and taking ~ talking and silence ~ here a
elsewhere ~ mountain and valley ~ river and sea ~ winter and summer ~ spring and fall ~ staying behind and going ahe
~ gentle and rough ~ mean and kind ~ false and true ~ evenness and unevenness ~ falling and rising ~ gold and silve
everywhere and nowhere ~ rest and restlessness ~ peace and war ~ body and soul ~ profit and loss ~ uselessness and usefuln
~ color and sound ~ flavor and taste ~ racing ahead and following behind ~ feelings and thoughts ~ that and this ~ disgra
and honor ~ luck and misfortune ~ pride and humility ~ above and below ~ bright and dark ~ form and formlessnes
image and illusion ~ time and space ~ suspicion and trust ~ temper and patience ~ selfishness and simplicity ~ yes and nc
dark and bright ~ same and different ~ yielding and resisting ~ virtue and vice ~ balance and falling over ~ heavy and ligh
stillness and unrest ~ care and abandonment ~ good and bad ~ being ahead and being behind ~ up and down ~ yielding ar
force ~ left and right ~ right and wrong ~ victory and defeat ~ poverty and wealth ~ shrinking and expanding ~ giving ar
receiving ~ soft and hard ~ weak and strong ~ just and unjust ~ dead and alive ~ laughter and tears ~ one and two ~ none ar
many ~ all and one ~ gaining and losing ~ fame and obscurity ~ softness and violence ~ anticipation and disappointment
reality and illusion ~ staying and leaving ~ letting be and interfering ~ shy and bold ~ humble and proud ~ old and young
deathless and dying ~ faith and disbelief ~ guiding and misleading ~ occupation and rest ~ harmony and discord ~ frien
and enemies ~ good and harm ~ honor and disgrace ~ rules and lawlessness ~ regulations and chaos ~ robbers and barror
~ calm and upheaval ~ honesty and fraud ~ good and evil ~ right and wrong ~ simple and intricate ~ cunning and slow
happiness and misery ~ honesty and dishonesty ~ goodness and witchcraft ~ giving up and giving in ~ great and sma
~ serving and being served ~ bitter and sweet ~ the tao and the ten thousand things ~ trust and suspicion ~ order and confusio
~ success and failure ~ holding on and letting go ~ few and many ~ same and different ~ brave and afraid ~ passionate an
indifferent ~ calm and restless ~ old and young ~ sick and healthy ~ servants and masters ~ weak and strong ~ hard and so
~ stiff and nimble ~ long and short ~ humility and pride ~ greatness and smallness ~ quarrels and agreements ~ resentmer
and appreciation ~ simple and complicated ~ abundance and scarcity ~ generosity and miserliness ~ numbers and lette
~ songs and speeches ~ ocean and desert ~ dry and wet ~ wrinkled and smooth ~ far and close ~ fire and water ~ dow
and up ~sad and happy ~ fast and slow ~ empty and full ~ master and disciple ~ living and dying ~ doubt and conviction
square and round ~ hot and cold ~ loud and quiet ~ question and answer ~ sad and happy ~ boredom and joy ~ lonely an
welcome ~ beginning and end ~ hope and hopelessness ~ freedom and imprisonment ~ tall and short ~ smart and dum
~ seldom and often ~ now and never ~ here and nowhere ~ nothing and everything ~ open and closed ~ fast and slow